The Witch's Revenge

Don't miss any of the chilling adventures!

Spooksville #1: *The Secret Path*

Spooksville #2: *The Howling Ghost*

Spooksville #3: *The Haunted Cave*

Spooksville #4: *Aliens in the Sky*

Spooksville #5: *The Cold People*

SPOOKSVILLE

THE WITCH'S
REVENGE

Christopher Pike

Aladdin

NEW YORK LONDON TORONTO SYDNEY NEW DELHI

This book is a work of fiction. Any references to historical events, real people, or real places are used fictitiously. Other names, characters, places, and events are products of the author's imagination, and any resemblance to actual events or places or persons, living or dead, is entirely coincidental.

ALADDIN

An imprint of Simon & Schuster Children's Publishing Division
1230 Avenue of the Americas, New York, NY 10020
First Aladdin edition February 2015
Copyright © 1996 by Christopher Pike
Cover illustration © 2015 by Vivienne To
All rights reserved, including the right of reproduction
in whole or in part in any form.
ALADDIN is a trademark of Simon & Schuster, Inc.,
and related logo is a registered trademark of Simon & Schuster, Inc.
For information about special discounts for bulk purchases,
please contact Simon & Schuster Special Sales at 1-866-506-1949
or business@simonandschuster.com.
Cover designed by Jessica Handelman
Interior designed by Mike Rosamilia
The text of this book was set in Weiss Std.
Manufactured in the United States of America 1215 OFF
4 6 8 10 9 7 5 3
This title has been cataloged with the Library of Congress.
ISBN 978-1-4814-1069-4 (pbk)
ISBN 978-1-4814-1071-7 (hc)
ISBN 978-1-4814-1073-1 (eBook)

THE ARGUMENT WAS OLD. WAS MS. ANN Templeton, Spooksville's most powerful and beautiful resident, a good witch or a bad witch? There was no question that she was a *real* witch. Adam Freeman and his friends had seen too many demonstrations of her power to doubt that. But whereas Adam and Watch liked to think she was a nice person, Sally Wilcox and Cindy Makey were certain she was dangerous.

The argument started in the Frozen Cow, Spooksville's best-known ice-cream parlor. Because the owner would serve only vanilla ice cream, they were each having a vanilla shake when the idea of visiting the witch's castle came up. Of course later they would blame each other for the idea. Later, that is, when they couldn't find their way out of the castle.

It was a hot summer Wednesday, ten in the morning, a perfect time for a milk shake. School was still a few weeks away. As often was the case, they were trying to decide what to do with the day.

"We can't go to the beach because of the sharks," Sally said as she listed the various possibilities. "We can't go to the lighthouse because we burned that down. We can't go to the reservoir because we burned that as well. And we can't go to the Haunted Cave because it's haunted." She paused. "Maybe we should try to contact Ekwee12 and go for another ride on a flying saucer."

Watch shook his head. "We forgot to get a communication device from him. We have no way to contact him."

"But he promised to call us someday," Adam said.

"Yes," Sally replied. "But he's an alien. They have a different perspective on time. Someday might be ten thousand years from now for him."

"I thought you didn't like Ekwee12," Cindy said to Sally. "You kept calling him Fat Head."

"I called him that because he had a fat head," Sally said. "That does not mean I disliked him. I call you plenty of names and I still like you." Sally added, "Most of the time."

Cindy was not impressed. "I am *so* relieved."

"What if we didn't do anything special today?" Adam suggested. "What if we just hung out and relaxed? We could play checkers or chess or something."

Sally stared at him as if he had lost his mind. "Are you all right, Adam?"

"I'm fine," he said. "Just because I want to have a relaxing day doesn't mean there's anything wrong with me."

"But this is Spooksville," Sally said. "We don't relax here. That's the best way to get yourself killed. You always have to be on your guard."

"I don't see how playing chess could be dangerous," Adam said. "Even in Spooksville."

"Ha," Sally said, turning to Watch. "Tell him what happened to Sandy Stone."

Watch frowned. "We're not sure if the game did it to her."

"Of course we are," Sally said. "She was playing on the witch's chess board when it happened."

"What happened to her?" Cindy asked.

Sally shrugged. "She turned to stone. What would you expect with a name like Sandy Stone?"

"Is that true?" Adam asked Watch.

Watch appeared uncertain. "Well, we did find a stone

statue of Sandy not far from the witch's castle. And the statue was sitting in front of a mysterious-looking chessboard."

"I don't understand," Cindy said.

"Chess was Sandy's favorite game," Sally explained. "She was a master at it. She could beat anyone in town. The trouble was, she boasted about the fact, and apparently Ms. Witch Ann Templeton heard about it and didn't like it. The witch plays chess herself, and sent out a challenge to Sandy, which Sandy accepted." Sally paused and shook her head. "And that was the last any of us saw her alive."

"Are you saying the witch turned her to stone because Sandy lost to her?" Adam asked.

"It may have been because Sandy beat the witch," Sally said. "The witch is a well-known sore loser."

"Is the stone statue still there?" Cindy asked.

"No," Watch said. "It was made of soft stone, like compressed sand. The first good storm and it was gone. Down the gutter."

Cindy glanced at Adam. "Do you believe this?" she asked.

Adam shrugged. "Ms. Ann Templeton never seemed that bad to me."

Sally snorted. "Just because she's pretty and smiled

at you, Adam, you're willing to forgive years of murder and genocide."

"What does genocide mean?" Adam asked Watch.

"Unpleasant behavior toward many people," Watch explained.

"I can't believe she'd murder anyone," Adam said.

Sally threw back her head and laughed. "You're too much! What about those friendly troll bodyguards of hers we met in her cellar? Have you forgotten how they tried to spear us for dinner? Do you think they were just playing? Do you think she didn't approve of their hunting habits?"

"But it was Ann Templeton who gave Bum and me clues about how to find you guys while you were trapped in the Haunted Cave," Watch said.

"Yeah," Adam said. "She also gave Watch the magic words that helped us rescue the Hyeet from the cave. How do you explain that?"

Sally replied with exaggerated patience. "She told Watch how to get into the cave because she figured there was no way he'd get out. She probably told him the magic word because she was hoping we'd all get trapped in another dimension."

"But when the Cold People attacked," Adam said, "she was one of the few people who really tried to fight them off."

"She was trying to save her own skin," Sally said. "Nothing else."

"For once I have to agree with Sally," Cindy said reluctantly. "I saw those trolls she keeps in her basement. She must be an evil witch to have such monsters in her castle."

"Not necessarily," Adam said. "She might just feel sorry for them. I imagine trolls have trouble finding places to live."

Sally stared at him. "I can't believe you just said that. Her castle may be many things, but it is not a home for homeless trolls."

"I've never actually seen her hurt anyone with my own eyes," Watch said.

"Yeah, but you're half blind," Sally said. "You've never actually seen the sun come up."

"I can see the sun," Watch said quietly, perhaps hurt by the remark. "I can see the moon, too, as long as I have my glasses on."

"A lot of these stories about people dying and disappearing," Adam said, "might have nothing to do with her. They might be caused by natural creatures, like aliens and ghosts and things."

"But if she isn't evil," Cindy said to Adam, "why is everyone so afraid of her?"

Adam shrugged. "People believe all kinds of nasty rumors." He added, "You know, she invited me to her castle once."

"But even you weren't dumb enough to accept her invitation," Sally said. "Which just proves my point. Deep inside you know she'd just as soon eat your heart out as smile at you."

"That's not true," Adam said. "The only reason I haven't visited her at her castle is because I've been too busy since I moved here."

"You're not busy today," Sally mocked.

"I wouldn't mind visiting her at her castle," Watch said softly, almost to himself. "I've heard she has the power to heal. I've always wondered if she could do anything about my eyes."

To everyone's surprise, Sally reached over and squeezed Watch's hand. "Your eyes are fine the way they are," she said. "You don't need to be healed by that witch. I shouldn't have said what I did about your vision. I'm sorry, Watch."

Cindy glanced at Adam. "I can't believe Sally just apologized," she said.

"I've seen her do it once before," Adam said.

Sally spoke seriously to all of them. "No one's going to the castle. There are alligators and crocodiles in her moat that would eat you alive before you could even get inside. Believe me, the place is a death trap."

"But there's a drawbridge," Watch said. "If she wants us to enter, she'll let it down."

Adam studied Watch. "You really do want to go, don't you? Do your eyes bother you that much?"

Watch looked away, out the window of the ice-cream parlor. "Well, you know, I don't like to complain."

"Complain," Adam said. "You're with friends. How are your eyes?"

"I don't know," Watch said. Briefly he removed his glasses and cleaned them on his shirt. When he put them back on, he squinted in the distance. "I think they're getting worse."

Cindy was concerned. "Can't you get stronger glasses?"

Watch spoke reluctantly. Clearly the subject embarrassed him. "The doctors say no. You see, it's not just a focusing problem. Everything seems to be getting dimmer, like it's always evening."

"How is it at nighttime?" Adam asked.

"I can't really see then at all," Watch said. "Not anymore. I just bump into things."

Sally was worried. "You never told us."

Watch shook his head. "There's nothing you guys can do."

"But you should have told Ekwee12," Cindy said. "Remember the way he fixed my ankle with his healing machine?"

"They weren't as bad then," Watch said. "And I didn't want to bother him."

"Watch," Adam said, frustrated. "He's our friend. He would have been happy to help you."

Watch lowered his head. "Well, he's gone now. And we don't know when he'll be coming back."

"But maybe Ann Templeton can help you," Adam said. "I think it's worth the risk to ask her. Why don't we do that now?"

"Do what?" Cindy asked.

"Go to the castle," Adam said simply.

Sally and Cindy looked at each other. "The boys have lost their minds," Sally said.

"They're looking for help in all the wrong places," Cindy agreed.

"You two don't have to come," Adam said. "If you're scared."

"I'm not scared," Sally said. "I am just a reasonable thinking human being. Calling on evil witches—even in the middle of the day—is just plain stupid. She won't heal Watch's eyes. More likely, she'll carve them out with one of her long red nails and have them in her evening soup."

"She wouldn't have such a terrible reputation if she hadn't done something bad," Cindy agreed.

"I trust my own instincts," Adam said. "I think she's a good witch. What do you say, Watch?"

Watch nodded enthusiastically. "I want to visit her. I think she'll welcome us, especially since she's already invited you."

"This is going to be a long day," Sally said darkly.

2

THE WALK TO ANN TEMPLETON'S CASTLE
was not long. The group had been near the place before,
of course. The castle was located on a hill overlooking
the cemetery. From its front gate one could see the
ocean as well. As they approached, Adam imagined that
Ann Templeton had a wonderful view up and down the
coast from the top of her highest tower.

From the outside, it appeared to be a medium-size
castle, but Adam knew from experience that its cellars
ran deep and many. Made of mostly large gray blocks
of stone, it was surrounded by a wide moat that at
first glance looked almost like a pleasant river. But if

one stared long enough, large dark shapes could be seen moving beneath the water's surface.

There was no doorknob or bell, and Adam wondered how they were supposed to make their presence known. He said as much to the others, but to Sally that was the least of their concerns.

"She knows we're here," Sally said. "No one gets near her place without her knowing."

Cindy gestured to the moat. "Has anybody ever fallen in there?"

"I have heard she pushed a few kids into the moat from the top of her tower," Sally said. "Their screams could be heard miles away."

Cindy turned to Adam. "I still think this is a bad idea," she said.

Adam was getting annoyed at the girls' gloomy outlook. "We told you that you and Sally should have stayed home."

"Yeah, but you accused us of being cowards," Sally said. "So in a sense you forced us to come."

Cindy jumped suddenly. "What's that?"

That was the sound of the drawbridge slowly being lowered. As a group they backed up. The wide wooden planks creaked as they descended; the metal gears sounded as if they hadn't been used in ages. Adam wondered if Ann Templeton normally used another route to exit the castle.

The drawbridge came to a dust-shaking halt a few feet in front of them. The boards it was made of were thick. Obviously it could support their weight. Yet as the drawbridge settled, they noticed that the crocodiles and the alligators swam closer. Adam saw several pairs of hungry eyes peering at him.

"She might try to raise it the second we step on it," Sally warned.

"We would slide off and straight into the water," Cindy agreed.

"I think she's welcoming us," Adam said, stepping onto the edge of the drawbridge. "I think it would be rude to ignore her welcome."

"Better to be rude than to be dead," Sally said.

Watch stepped all the way onto the bridge. "I don't care about the rest of you. I'm going to talk to her."

Adam stopped him. "Before we go inside, I want you to know there's probably only a small chance she can help with your eyes. I mean, I just don't want you to get your hopes up."

Watch smiled faintly. "I know that, Adam. You don't have to worry about me. I always get by."

Sally looked at Cindy. "Stop them."

"How am I supposed to stop them?" Cindy asked.

"I don't know," Sally said. "You always get Adam to do what you want."

"Adam, don't go inside," Cindy said. "Please."

"I have to go," Adam said. He tugged on Watch's arm with the four watches he always wore. "Come on, we'll go alone. There's no reason to risk the girls."

Cindy turned to Sally. "That didn't work."

Sally caught up to Adam. "No reason to risk the girls? There you go again, another sexist statement. Cindy and I can take whatever risks you take."

"I wish you wouldn't drag me into your feminist philosophy," Cindy said, even though she had also hurried to catch up to them.

The front door was huge. If the four of them had stood on one another's shoulders, they still wouldn't have been able to reach the top. There was no doorbell, only a huge, gold skull-shaped door knocker. Sally didn't like the design.

"When have you ever seen a skull on the door of a good witch?" she said.

"It's decorative," Adam said, reaching up to use it. He knocked gently a couple of times, and then took a step back. He didn't know what sort of creature would answer the door, or if it would be Ann Templeton herself. But he was assuming somebody would answer. That was why he was so surprised when the door slowly began to swing open by itself. As a group, they stared into the vast dark interior. They could see a fire burning in a grate in the distance, little else.

"Hello," Adam called.

His word echoed as it trailed off into the distance.

No one called back.

"Could the castle be empty?" Cindy wondered out loud.

"If it's empty, then who opened the door?" Watch said.

"It could be a magic door," Sally said.

"I don't think the place is empty," Adam said. "You don't just go and leave a castle without someone to guard it." He gestured to the open door. "I think we're being invited inside."

"Why isn't she here to make the invitation in person?" Sally said. "This feels like a setup to me. As soon as we step inside, the door will close behind us. Then the trolls will come, and we'll be dead meat."

Adam stuck his head through the open door. Besides the distant fireplace, he could now make out a row of burning torches lighting a long hallway. But the actual walls of the room, the furniture it may have contained— that was hidden in the shadows.

"I don't see any trolls," Adam muttered.

"You don't see a butler in a tuxedo either," Sally said. "This is too weird. I say we turn around now, have another vanilla shake at the Frozen Cow, and consider ourselves lucky we listened to me."

Watch stepped forward. "I've been in darker places. I don't mind doing a little exploring."

Adam followed him. "If she wanted to hurt us, she could have hurt us already."

Sally chased after them. "If she wants to hurt you, you don't have to make it easy for her."

Cindy also followed them inside. "We don't even have a flashlight," she fretted.

They were barely inside when the door slammed shut at their backs.

The noise made them jump.

"I'm not going to say I told you so," Sally whispered in the dark. "But I did."

THE ENTRY ROOM WAS VAST, WITH WALLS OF rough gray stone. As their eyes adjusted to the dim light cast by the fireplace and the torches in the nearby hall, Adam saw that the room was empty. There was no furniture, and no ornaments or paintings of any kind. He wondered if Ann Templeton ever came into this room. Although it was free of dust and other signs of age, it felt as if it had been deserted for a long time.

"It's cold in here," Cindy said, shivering.

"It is a psychic chill you feel," Sally said. "Your soul realizes it has entered a place of great evil, from which there is no escape."

"I kind of like this place," Watch said, squinting into the dark.

"It's good to be out of the sun," Adam agreed.

"You guys are in a state of denial," Sally snapped. "We're already in danger and you refuse to admit it. Where is Ms. Ann Templeton? She knows we're here. The only reason she hasn't appeared is because she's playing some weird game with us. And her games are always dangerous."

"I wouldn't mind leaving now," Cindy said, glancing around nervously.

"I want to see what's at the end of this hallway," Adam said, gesturing to the torch-lit passageway. With Watch, he stepped into the narrow stone hallway. The girls followed a few steps behind, whispering about how stupid boys are.

"Can you see where you're going?" Adam asked Watch.

"I'm okay," his friend said. "Do you think she's here?"

"She must be here," Adam said.

"I hope we meet her before we run into one of her trolls," Watch said.

"I think she keeps them in the basement," Adam said.

"I wonder what else she keeps there," Watch said.

The hallway was long. It wound left then right. Finally they entered another large room. This one was also lit by torches and a single massive fireplace, but it was decorated as a castle chamber should be, with oversize gilt furniture, and massive paintings of forgotten battles. There was even a gem-encrusted throne at the far end of the room. But that wasn't what caught their eyes first.

In the center of the chamber was a huge hourglass.

In place of sand, sparkling jewel dust drifted slowly downward.

The dust glowed like stars as it counted off the seconds.

"We've seen this before," Adam said, touching the hourglass. It was twice their height and supported by a shiny stand made of gold and silver.

"Where?" Cindy asked.

"On the other side of the Secret Path," Sally said. "In the evil witch's castle. We didn't tell you about her, but she was a real pain. Except on the other side of the Secret Path the sand flowed upward—probably because time flowed backward in that dimension." Sally paused. "In fact, the evil witch said that Ann Templeton had a similar hourglass. It was as if she wanted us to know. Do you guys remember?"

"I do," Watch said. "I also remember that her evil sister's hourglass was the main source of her power."

Sally rested her palm on the hourglass, her face lit with color from the sparkling dust. "I wonder if this is the source of Ann Templeton's power," she said, a mischie-vous note in her voice. "If we hold it all in our hands."

"I think you two are forgetting something," Adam said. "When we broke the other hourglass, the whole place went crazy. Everything started to fall apart. We have to be careful with this hourglass. Who knows what would happen to our world if we damaged it."

"I wasn't thinking of breaking it," Sally said.

"We believe you," Watch said.

"It's incredibly beautiful," Cindy said. "I wonder what this sand is made of. It looks like stardust."

"It might be *real* stardust," Watch said. "It definitely has some kind of power."

"But that brings me back to my original questions," Sally said. "Why does she let us find these things? Why isn't she here to explain what we're looking at? I still think this is some kind of setup. We have to be careful."

Adam pointed to another narrow hallway. "Let's check down there."

"If we take hallway after hallway," Cindy warned. "We'll end up lost."

"She has a point," Sally said. "You notice we haven't really gone underground, and yet we've already covered a lot of ground, more ground than the castle seems to cover from the outside."

"What are you saying?" Adam asked.

Sally spoke seriously. "We might be in another dimension already, and not know it."

"I think you're jumping to your usual grim conclusions," Watch said.

"We'll see," Sally said.

They walked down the next hallway and into another room. This one was not so large as the previous one, nor were there as many decorations or furniture. But there was another blazing fireplace. With all the fires, Adam wondered why the castle wasn't permanently shrouded in smoke on the outside. Yet despite the fires, the room was as cold as the others.

In the center of this chamber were four necklaces. They rested on a white sheet. From each necklace hung a single colored precious stone: a green emerald, a red ruby, a blue sapphire, a yellow topaz. The jewels were exquisite, perfectly polished and large. Adam figured they must be worth a fortune. Each one was attached to a fine gold band. The gold also wrapped around each stone, like a miniature claw, and held the gems in place. In front of each necklace was a small card with a single printed word on it.

Before the emerald was the word IMMORTALITY.

Beside the ruby was the word STRENGTH.

In front of the sapphire was the word MATURITY.

Next to the yellow topaz the card said BEAUTY.

The stones seemed to shimmer with a light of their own making. As the four of them approached, they found they could not stop staring at the gems. Adam in particular was drawn to the blue sapphire. He didn't know why, but he felt as if Ann Templeton had laid it out specially for him. Being on the short side for his age, he had always wanted to be older, more mature. He had no doubt that each stone was capable of giving the quality listed beside it. For some reason, he immediately assumed they were magical necklaces.

Adam went to touch the sapphire when Sally stopped him.

"Don't," she said. "It's a trap."

Adam had to blink to clear his head. He realized that in a space of a few seconds the stones had almost hypnotized him. "What are you talking about?" he asked.

"She wants us to put these on," Sally said.

"I don't want to put one of them on," Cindy said.

Sally eyed her suspiciously. "Aren't you attracted to one of them, Cindy?"

Cindy seemed embarrassed. "Well, the yellow topaz looks nice."

"Which one do you like, Watch?" Sally asked.

"The red ruby," Watch said.

"Adam?" Sally said.

"I like the blue one," Adam said. "But so what?"

"I like the green emerald," Sally said. "I was immediately drawn to it. Like you, I started to reach out and put it on. But then I remembered where I was, who I was dealing with." She paused. "These have been placed here to tempt each of us. They were designed to do that."

"I still don't know what you're talking about," Cindy said.

"The witch knows us," Sally said. "She can probably read our minds. For example, she knows that you, Cindy, are obsessed with your appearance."

Cindy was insulted. "That's ridiculous! I'm not vain."

"You're as vain as a Persian cat," Sally said. "You're not attracted to the topaz because you like the stone. You like the idea of what it can do for you. Listen, I'm not singling you out. You guys are always talking about how obsessed I am with death. Well, what I'm really interested in is living forever."

"Sally might have a point," Adam said. "I'm drawn to the sapphire, and I think it's because it can make me older and wiser."

Cindy shook her head. "It never occurred to me to want to look more beautiful."

"Fine," Sally said. "Then there's no need for you to try on the topaz necklace."

"I can try it on if I want," Cindy said.

Sally snorted. "I bet you put it on the second I look away."

"You might have a point," Watch said. "I am drawn to the ruby. If it gives me strength, maybe it will make my eyes and ears stronger as well. I want to try it on. I think I'm going to in a second, just to see if it works."

Sally was exasperated. "Are you crazy? You think we'll get these qualities for free? The witch will make us pay for whatever these stones can do for us."

"How do we know they can do anything for us?" Cindy interrupted. "They might just be pretty pieces of jewelry."

"Because we're in a witch's castle," Sally said. "Not a shopping mall. The witch has magic, I never said she didn't. But it's black magic. I say we get out of here now."

"Which you've said before," Adam muttered.

"Good advice cannot be repeated too often," Sally said.

"But if we leave now," Watch warned, "we'll never know what these necklaces might do for us." He reached for the ruby. "I'll try this one on. Just me. The rest of you watch and see if anything happens to me."

Sally quickly grabbed his arm. "No! What if you turn into a frog?"

"I have never seen a strong frog," Cindy remarked.

"Maybe she does want to trick us," Watch said to Sally, who continued to hold on to his arm. "But maybe she wants to help us. We've had this argument already. The only way we can know is for one of us to put on one of these necklaces." He reached down and gently removed Sally's fingers. "Don't worry, if I turn into something gross you can always put me in the creek. I sort of like it there anyway."

Sally shook her head and took a step back. "It's your life."

"And I'm not getting any younger," Watch agreed.

He reached down and put the ruby necklace over his head.

He paused and looked around, blinking several times.

The rest of them held their breath.

"Interesting," Watch finally muttered.

"Do you feel strong?" Adam asked.

Watch flexed his arms, squeezed his fingers.

"I feel slightly different," he said.

"But do you feel stronger?" Sally demanded.

Watch continued to flex his muscles, to look around. "Yes. I feel just a tiny bit stronger. And I think I can see slightly better."

"You might just be imagining the changes," Cindy warned.

Watch stretched out his arms and took a few steps around the room. "I don't think so. I could barely see this room at all a few seconds ago. Now I can see the walls, the details on the stone work." He paused. "The effect is growing as time passes. Already I can see better than when I first put on the necklace."

Adam laughed nervously. "If you keep getting stronger, your muscles will bulge out of your clothes."

Watch smiled, which he rarely did. He fingered the necklace lovingly. "I like this. I think you guys should try on the other ones."

Cindy reached for the topaz. "All right. But I can't imagine that I could look any more beautiful than I already do."

Sally grabbed her arm. "Wait a second! This hasn't been long enough for an experiment. We have to watch Watch longer to see how he changes."

Cindy shook her off. "But we can already see that the change is for the better. If I want to try on the necklace, I can. You're not the boss, you know."

"I should be," Sally said.

"Maybe I should be the next one to try on a necklace," Adam said, staring at the sapphire again. "Let us guys take the risks."

"Ha," Cindy said. "Let you guys get to enjoy all the magic is what you mean. Let's try on the necklaces together. That's only fair."

Sally continued to shake her head. "You're all going to turn into toads. I'm going to have to go down to the creek every day just to see you."

Adam and Cindy ignored her. Together they put on the necklaces they were most drawn to. Adam liked the feel of it as it went around his neck. He stroked the sapphire as it hung close to his heart. He glanced over at Cindy, who was beaming at him.

"How do I look?" she asked.

"The same," Sally muttered. "Like a stick in the mud."

"No," Watch said, stepping closer to Cindy. "I think you look better. Adam?"

Adam studied Cindy. "Yeah. She looks more radiant. Like she's glowing."

Cindy grinned and rubbed her bare arms. "I feel more beautiful. I feel—it's hard to describe—like I'm filling up with light."

"I feel like I'm getting a headache," Sally moaned. "How about you, Adam? Are you older and wiser?"

Adam frowned. "It's like Cindy said. It's hard to describe. I feel some kind of change—a little stronger, a little smarter maybe."

"I think you look a little taller," Watch said.

"Yeah, he's definitely not as short," Cindy said enthusiastically.

Adam was taken aback. "I didn't know you thought I was short."

Cindy patted his shoulder. "I didn't mean you were short short. You just weren't . . . as tall as Watch." She paused and burst out laughing. "But what does it matter now? You're going to be taller than all of us. Hey, Sally, go ahead, put on your necklace."

"Yeah," Adam said. "If it does work, and it makes you immortal, then nothing's going to hurt you anyway. What do you have to lose?"

Sally glanced at the emerald necklace. "Are you sure you guys feel better?"

Cindy began to dance about the room. "I feel like a beautiful princess. I *am* a princess!"

"I can definitely see better," Watch said, taking off his glasses.

"And I definitely feel less like a kid," Adam said.

Sally reached out and touched the necklace, but then withdrew her hand. "But don't you like feeling like a kid?" she asked.

"I think these necklaces are gifts," Adam said simply.

"I guess I'll have to trust you guys," Sally said.

And with that she reached down and lifted the emerald necklace and placed it over her head. For a moment she stood fingering the beautiful green stone. Then she looked up and let out a laugh.

"Now I feel more like a kid," she exclaimed.

Another wave of laughter sounded, but it didn't come from any of them. This laughter was older, deeper, darker, and maybe a little wicked. It came from the direction of a hallway that none of them had noticed because it had been unlit. But now a tall figure in a black cloak was walking their way, a burning torch in her hand. Her green eyes glimmered even before she entered the room, and Adam was reminded of the emerald in Sally's magical necklace. For right then Adam was convinced they were in the presence of great magic. But whether it was white or black, he wasn't yet sure.

"It's the witch," Sally whispered, scared.

"Shh," Adam warned. "Don't call her that."

"But I don't mind," Ann Templeton said as she stepped into the room and threw back her cape. She smiled as she said it, even laughed, but in her green eyes was a light more dangerous than any they had seen before. It was cold as the glow of a frosty dawn but as powerful as the light from a distant star. She added, "I'm your favorite witch."

4

"WHAT DO YOU WANT?" SALLY ASKED SUS-
piciously. Instinctively, they had all gathered together.
Cindy was, in fact, holding on to Adam's arm. They
even backed up a step as Ann Templeton came farther
into the room. She was as Adam remembered, beautiful
with her long dark hair and piercing green eyes. She was
also as pale as he recalled; it didn't seem as if she often
saw the sun. She smiled slyly at Sally's question, as she
stood tall and in command in front of them.

"Shouldn't I be the one to ask that question?" she
said. "You four are the ones, after all, who came here
looking for something."

"We don't want anything from you," Sally snapped.

Ann Templeton was amused. "Oh, Sally, then why have you tried to steal my necklaces?"

Adam stuttered. "We didn't intend to steal anything, ma'am. We just wanted to try them on. We can put them back now if you want."

Ann Templeton continued to wear a smile. "Do you think you can just put them back, Adam?" she asked. "Do you honestly think it's that simple?"

"I'll put mine back if you don't want me to have it," Watch said. He took hold of the necklace and began to pull it over his head. "We thought maybe they were gifts, but we're sorry if we made a mistake."

Then Watch froze, the necklace halfway over his head.

He looked stunned.

"What is it?" Sally asked nervously.

"I can't get it off," Watch said.

"What do you mean you can't get it off?" Sally asked. "Just take it off."

"You try taking yours off," Watch said.

Sally reached down and started to pull the necklace over her head. But she could only get it halfway over. The fine gold band refused to pass all the way over her head.

"Oh no," Sally whispered.

Adam and Cindy tried to take off their necklaces. But they couldn't get them over their heads.

Ann Templeton laughed softly to herself.

"Do you still think it's that simple?" she asked.

Sally took a step forward. "You tricked us."

Ann Templeton shook her head. "No. You tricked yourselves. I didn't make you put on the necklaces. If you had come here not wanting anything, you wouldn't be in this situation right now."

"Are we in trouble?" Adam asked. "I mean, I kind of like this necklace. If it's stuck around my head, I don't mind." He added, "As long as you don't mind that I keep it?"

Ann Templeton stared at him. "That is sweet of you to say so, Adam. Actually, I made these necklaces for each of you. Certainly you can keep them. If you meet just one condition."

"What is that?" Sally asked suspiciously.

"My condition is simple," Ann Templeton said. "You just have to find your way out of my castle. If you do, then you can keep your necklace. You'll even be able to take it off and put it back on whenever you wish." She added in a more menacing tone, "But as long as you're in my castle, you won't be able to take off the necklace. No matter how hard you try."

"But we know how to get out of here," Watch said. "We just have to walk back to the hourglass room, and then through the hallway on the right, and then we'll come back to the front gate."

"Where is the hourglass room?" Ann Templeton asked in a slightly mocking tone.

"It's just over . . . ," Watch began, before his voice trailed into silence.

The hallway through which they had entered into the room was gone.

"Am I confused?" Watch asked Adam.

Adam shook his head. "No. The hallway's vanished. It must have disappeared while we were putting on the necklaces."

"It disappeared the moment all four of you had your necklaces on," Ann Templeton said.

"It's just as I thought," Sally said bitterly. "This has all been a setup to trap us. I told you guys she was an evil witch."

Sally's outburst caused Ann Templeton to laugh heartily. "The necklaces are not here to trap you, Sally. They're here to test you."

"How?" Watch asked.

"You will see," Ann Templeton said as she turned to leave. "Now I have to get back to my own affairs. I will give you only one piece of advice while you stumble around trying to find your way out of here." She paused. "Watch out for my boys."

Cindy gulped. "Who are your boys?"

Ann Templeton smiled. "My boys are like boys everywhere. Full of fun and mischief. But their ideas of fun might not be the same as yours." She laughed at that. "Try to stay out of their way!"

With that Ann Templeton strode back up the hallway from which she had emerged. As her torch began to fade in the long darkness, they noticed that the opening to the hallway had vanished. Leaving them trapped in a room that had no exit.

5

"NOW WHAT ARE WE GOING TO DO?" SALLY grumbled.

"She said this is a test," Adam said. "That means there must be a way out of this room. What do you say, Watch?"

Watch continued to flex his arms and hands. "I hope it's true. But if it's not, it won't matter if I keep growing stronger. Soon I'll be able to tear down these walls."

Adam nodded as he studied his own body. The floor definitely looked farther away. "I'm changing fast as well," he said. "I think I must be thirteen years old by now."

Sally, who looked an inch shorter, made a sarcastic swooning sound. "Oh, an older man. How exciting."

"I'm not ready to panic yet," Cindy said. "I'm still excited about my necklace." She paused. "I wish I had a mirror. Do I look as pretty as I feel?"

"You look very nice," Adam said honestly.

Sally squinted at Cindy. "I don't know if you're prettier or not, Cindy. But I think you're beginning to glow. I mean really glow, like a lightbulb."

It was true. As Cindy stepped away from the fireplace and into the shadows, she seemed to cast a shadow of her own. Her skin was emitting a faint radiance, almost as if she were radioactive. But the effect didn't disturb Cindy. She appeared excited about it.

"I can be a movie star," she said. "I don't just have sparkle in my eyes. I have it everywhere!"

"Do I need to remind you that we are in a life-and-death situation here?" Sally said in a slightly squeaky voice. "We are surrounded by stone walls, and have nothing to eat or drink."

Watch gestured to the ceiling. He had been staring at it for the last minute. "I think I see a hole into the attic."

"What are you talking about?" Adam said. "I don't see anything."

"And castles don't have attics," Sally added.

"It doesn't matter what we call it," Watch said,

removing his glasses and rubbing his eyes, before point-ing to one spot on the dark stone ceiling. "It looks like a way out to me."

"But we could never get up there," Cindy said.

In response, Watch jumped off the floor. But it wasn't an ordinary jump that an ordinary boy might make. He flew up at least six feet before coming back down.

"Wow," he said. "I can't wait till the next Olympics. I'll clean up on the gold medals."

"But even if you're feeling stronger," Sally said. "That ceiling's thirty feet high. You can't reach it."

Adam gestured to the table where they had found the necklaces. "But what if we take this table, break it in half, and set the two halves on top of each other? If Watch jumped from the top of that, he might be able to reach the hole in the ceiling."

"But what about us?" Cindy asked. "We'll still be stuck."

Watch pulled the long white sheet off the tabletop. "I'll take this with me. And once I'm up there, I'll lower it for Adam to grab. And you two can hold on to Adam's feet and I'll pull you all up at once."

Sally smirked. "Right. You can lift all of us at once."

Watch spoke with a straight face. "I think I can. I know for sure I can bust this table into two pieces. Stand aside, I don't want any of you to get hurt."

To their amazement, they watched as Watch cut the table in half with one sharp karate chop. Or perhaps Adam was not that surprised. It had been his idea to begin with, and he was growing smarter all the time, not to mention taller.

Not needing their help, Watch piled the one piece of the table on top of the other. Then he tucked the tablecloth in his belt and jumped up on the very top of the tables. The gang moved back even farther as he made a desperate leap for the hole in the ceiling. His first effort failed, and he came crashing back down on the tabletop. The wood shuddered, as if he weighed a ton, and they feared the whole structure would come crashing down.

But Watch wasn't fazed. He made another superhuman leap, and this time he managed to catch the rim of the hole. In two seconds he had pulled himself up and out of view. But his head reappeared a moment later.

"This hole is like a heating duct," he called down. "It looks like it goes way back." He began to feed the edge of the sheet down. "Hurry, grab hold of the cloth. We should get out of here before Ann Templeton comes back."

"But what if you drop us?" Sally asked as she climbed up on the split tabletop.

"You're the last person who has to worry about that," Watch said. "You're immortal now."

Sally frowned. "I don't know about that. I just feel . . ." She suddenly stopped. "Hey, is my voice getting higher?"

"Yeah," Cindy said. "And you're getting shorter, too."

"You're not just getting shorter," Adam said, studying Sally. "You're getting younger."

Sally was stunned. "You mean you guys get to be older and stronger and more beautiful? And I have to turn into a baby?"

"Looks like it," Adam said. "But I'm not surprised the witch gave you the worst necklace. You're always rude to her."

"Right now we don't know which necklace is good," Watch warned from above them. "And which necklace might be bad."

Cindy giggled. "I'm not worried about becoming too beautiful."

Sally gave her a hard look. "I think we should all be worried."

The three of them finished climbing up on the second of the tabletops. But it was only Adam—who was now taller than the rest of them by three inches—who could reach the sheet Watch had fed down. For that reason, Sally and Cindy did end up having to hold on to

Adam's legs as Watch pulled them up. It was a strange sensation, Adam thought, to have his friend slowly tug him into the air as if he were a balloon while the girls clung on to his ankles.

"That wasn't so bad," Adam said, when they were all huddled in the hole in the ceiling. Below them they could still see the massive fireplace and the many burning torches. Too late he realized they should have brought one of the torches with them. The hole Watch had lifted them into looked long and dark.

"It's too bad we don't have a flashlight," Cindy said, peering into the dark.

"I don't think I need one," Watch said, as he put his glasses in his pocket. "My eyes are getting more sensitive with each passing minute. I can practically see in the dark."

They crawled forward, with Watch leading the way, Cindy behind him, Sally behind her, and Adam bringing up the rear. The tunnel wasn't level. For a while it headed down, then back up. It seemed as if they had crawled forever when Watch finally told them to halt. Adam thought he heard metal scraping across stone, but he could not see his friend at the front of their group.

"There is some kind of grid over the space in front of us," Watch said.

"Does it look like a way out?" Sally asked.

"It might be," Watch said. "But I can't see any floor below it. I think it would be risky to jump down." He paused and sniffed the air. "There's this strange smell coming from below the grid."

"What's it smell like?" Cindy asked.

"I'm not sure," Watch said. "But it's not pleasant."

"Can the grid support our weight?" Sally asked.

"That's another reason I stopped," Watch said. "It's pretty rusty. I think we better go over it onc at a time."

"Good," Sally said. "You go first."

Adam heard Watch moving onto the edge of the grid. The metal creaked loudly, and Adam realized his heart was pounding. "Be careful, Watch," he whispered.

"It's bending," Watch said in a tight voice. "We'll be lucky if we all get across."

"Well, don't bend it too much," Sally said. "I don't want to be trapped in here the rest of my life. Especially when it was not my idea to come at all."

"I thought you weren't going to say I told you so," Adam said.

"It goes without saying," Sally replied.

"I'm almost to the other side of the grid," Watch whispered.

"How far across is it?" Adam asked.

"A long ten feet," Watch called back. He seemed

to shift in the darkness ahead of them, perhaps turning around. "There, I've made it. Come, Cindy, but be sure to move slowly."

"I'm scared," Cindy whispered as she moved onto the grid. Once more Adam heard the creaking metal. "What if it breaks?"

"Then you will probably fall screaming to your death," Sally said in her most helpful manner.

"You won't die," Adam said in an encouraging tone. "You're a beautiful princess. The beautiful princess never dies in fairy tales."

"The only trouble with that analogy is that Spooksville is as far from a fairy-tale setting as you can get," Sally said.

"Would you shut up?" Cindy hissed. "You're making me nervous."

"How do you think I feel?" Sally asked. "I have to go after you and Watch have bent the grid all out of shape."

"I can hardly wait until you regress to an infant," Cindy muttered. "To before you could talk."

Adam sighed. "Isn't it amazing how we all band together at the times of greatest danger?"

Cindy made it across. They heard her celebrating on the other side with Watch. Now it was Sally's turn, and she, too, sounded scared as she crawled onto the grid.

"It smells like death down there," she whispered.

"Try not to look down," Adam said.

"Try telling that to my nose," Sally said, obviously sweating every inch that she crawled over the grid. For Adam, she was a moving blur—even though he was only a few feet behind her. The darkness seemed to press down upon all of them as the stink below grew stronger.

Adam thought he heard something moving far below. Wicked licking sounds.

He prayed the grid didn't break when it was his turn.

Finally, he heard Sally call from up ahead.

"I made it," she said. "Just pretend you're as light as a hot air balloon, Adam, and you'll have no problem."

"The only problem with that is I think I've gained twenty pounds in the last five minutes," Adam said, feeling for the edge of the grid. "I wonder how old I am now."

"I wonder when you'll stop aging," Watch said darkly.

Adam moved onto the grid. Immediately it sagged way down. It was unfortunate—if he had been his normal size and weight, the grid would have supported him fine. Now it was creaking painfully. It sounded as if its many metal wires were desperately straining to hold together. Adam felt desperate. There was definitely something moving far below, and it didn't sound human. Adam could hear the creature licking its chops, as if expecting a fresh meal. Had the witch just given the necklace to make him into a bigger piece of meat? It was a terrifying thought.

"You're almost there," Sally whispered on the other side.

"I've barely climbed onto the blasted thing," Adam whispered back.

"I know that," Sally said. "I was just trying to be supportive."

The grid suddenly let out a loud creak.

It dropped down a whole foot.

"Adam!" Cindy screamed.

"I'm still here," Adam gasped, trembling badly. He was clutching the metal for dear life, barely able to squeeze his fingers between the interlaced metal strips. Behind him, he believed, the grid had already torn loose. If he were to let go for a second, he knew he would slide off into the creature's lair. Clearly there was no chance of going back.

"You have to move carefully," Watch advised.

"But you have to hurry up and do it," Sally said. "I can feel the edge of the grid on this side. It's ready to pull away."

Adam could feel the grid slowly sinking beneath him. He feared if he moved it would just collapse. "I think I'm stuck," he said softly. "I think this is it."

"Hang on," Sally pleaded. "I have a plan."

"I'm all ears," Adam whispered, feeling the sweat drip into his eyes, the perspiration sliding over his palms, making them slippery.

"Watch," Sally said. "Do you still have the sheet you used to pull us up here with?"

"Sure." There was a rustling in the dark. "Are you going to throw it down to him?"

"Yes," Sally said. "Adam, in a moment you'll probably feel the sheet on your face or on your hands. Grab hold of it and we'll pull you up."

"Are you pulling me up or is Watch?" Adam wanted to know.

"Watch can't squeeze past Cindy to get to where I'm sitting," Sally said. "It'll have to be me. But don't worry, I'm stronger than I look."

"For a five-year-old," Cindy muttered.

"I'm not five yet," Sally snapped.

"You sound like it," Cindy said.

Adam felt the edge of the sheet brush the side of his face. "Are you sure you can hold me?" he asked. "I'm going to make a grab for the sheet right now."

"I'll try my best," Sally said. "Cindy, you hold on to me. Watch, you hold on to Cindy."

"We'll probably all end up going over the edge," Cindy muttered.

"I'm going to do it now," Adam said again.

"We're ready for you," Sally whispered, tense.

In a single swift move, Adam let go of the grill with his right hand and grabbed at the sheet. He could feel exactly where it was, lying against his cheek, and had no trouble getting hold of it. The only problem was that his sudden move made the grill sink even deeper. He had one hand on the grill and the other on the sheet and if he let go of either he was sure he was doomed.

"Can you pull me up?" he gasped.

"Can't you crawl up?" Sally gasped back. It sounded as if she was straining as hard as she could to support him.

"I don't know," Adam said, feeling himself slip slowly down, inch by inch. "Can't you help, Watch?"

"Unfortunately the sheet isn't long enough," Watch said. "Whatever you're going to do, you'd better do it now. I don't think Sally can hang on much longer."

"Ain't that the truth," Sally whispered.

Using the taut sheet for support, Adam desperately tried to pull himself up. But now the grid was a mass of scary creaks. Adam could actually hear the individual wires snapping as the grid sank so low that for all practical purposes it was hanging straight down. Far below, the waiting creature seemed to giggle. A wave of putrid air floated upward, making Adam feel faint.

"I can't hold on," he cried.

"You have to," Sally said. "You can't die just when I've become immortal. I'll be bored for the rest of eternity without you to bother."

Both the sheet and the grid were slowly slipping from his hands. "I can't do it," he moaned. "I'm falling."

"You fall and I'll kill you," Sally said anxiously.

"You have to try harder," Cindy pleaded.

"Just make one big jump for us," Watch said. "It's your only chance."

"All right," Adam said as he struggled for air. "I'm doing it on the count of three. One . . . Two . . . Three!"

Using both his arms, Adam yanked up as hard as he could. Unfortunately, the edge of the grid was too far gone to take the shock. Still, he almost made it. He was actually able to grab hold of Sally's hand. He grabbed it hard, as if his life depended on it, which it did. But in a way it made the situation worse.

The whole grid gave way.

It fell crashing below.

There was a high-pitched cry from below—the complaint of an inhuman monster.

Adam dangled in midair, clutching the sheet with one hand, and Sally's hand with the other. Above him, he could feel Sally being pulled over the edge.

"I have to let go!" he cried.

"I won't let go of you!" Sally screamed.

"You must!" Adam shouted. "You'll be pulled over the edge with me."

"No!" Sally cried.

But Adam was right. He was already doomed, and because Sally refused to let him fall, she, too, was pulled over the edge. The tension broke all at once. The two of them had been fighting with every last drop of strength they had, then suddenly they were falling—into a black abyss where a pair of hungry red eyes waited to eat them alive.

6

CINDY AND WATCH SAT IN DARKNESS, INSIDE
and out. Neither could comprehend what had just happened. The shock was too great. Sally and Adam—their
best friends—were just gone. Everything in the world
seemed hopeless.

"Can you see anything?" Cindy whispered to Watch
as she knelt at the edge of the torn grill.

"I'm having trouble seeing past you," Watch said. "But
it wouldn't matter if I was sitting where you're sitting."

Cindy's voice cracked. "Because they're dead already?"

Watch spoke heavily. "I'm afraid so. They couldn't
have survived that fall, or whatever it is that's down
there."

Cindy winced. "Do you think it's going to eat them?"

"We shouldn't think about that. They're already beyond feeling pain."

Cindy felt cold tears wash over her face. "We should never have come to this evil place. I didn't want to come."

"I know and you were right," Watch said. "It was my fault. I was just worried about myself." He sighed. "And now I've killed my best friends."

Cindy patted his arm. "You can't blame yourself. You just wanted to be able to see better. There's nothing wrong with that."

Watch hung his head. "I would trade both my eyes just to see Adam once again, and to hear Sally's voice."

After sitting for a few more minutes in mourning, they continued to crawl through the stone tunnel. There was nothing else they could do. Cindy wept as they crawled, but Watch kept his tears inside, where he kept most emotions.

After maybe twenty minutes of plugging along, they found that the passageway took a sharp turn downward. Fortunately metal rungs appeared on the sides, and they were able to grasp them for support. Pretty soon they were climbing straight down, as if they were on a ladder. As they descended the temperature increased. A faint red glow appeared below and it seemed as if they were coming to the end of the passageway.

"We've been going down for a long time," Cindy said as they paused to catch their breath. "That's not good. We must have entered the witch's basements. That's where we ran into the trolls before."

Watch nodded, clinging to the metal rungs below her. "I'm sure when she was talking about her boys, she meant the trolls. Do you think it's possible she told the trolls not to eat us?"

"I doubt it," Cindy said bitterly. "It was she who forced us to crawl through this stone hole. I blame her for Adam and Sally's deaths. When we get out of here, I'm going straight to the police to report her."

"The police won't do anything about it," Watch said. "They're afraid of Ann Templeton." He shook his head as he stared down below them. "I really didn't think she'd do anything to hurt us."

"Sally was wiser than all of us," Cindy said in a sad voice. "And I was always so mean to her."

"You were never mean to her," Watch said. "You were just always annoyed with her." He gestured to the red light below them. "We can't hang here forever. We're going to have to try our luck with the trolls. I just wish we had a weapon of some kind."

"Do you think you're strong enough to beat up one yet?" Cindy asked.

"No matter how strong I get," Watch said, "I don't think I'll be able to take a spear in the chest." He paused and stared at her. "You keep getting brighter. We're going to have trouble hiding you from the trolls."

Cindy studied her body. Watch was right, with each passing minute the flesh on her arms and legs was shining with more light. Indeed, it was almost as if her skin were becoming transparent.

"If it comes down to it," she said, "you save yourself. Don't try to save me as well."

Watch shook his head. "Did you see how Sally refused to let go of Adam? She held on to him even though she knew it would kill her. How can I leave you behind?"

Cindy wiped away another tear. "She was very brave."

They climbed down the remainder of the passageway. The dull red light was their guide. As they climbed out, they found themselves in a wide stone cave. It stretched out in both directions and appeared empty. But the red light was only coming from the right. The left was completely dark.

"This reminds me of the Haunted Cave," Cindy said.

"But it isn't," Watch said. "We're not that deep. This tunnel was dug."

"But that's an idea," Cindy said. "If we could go even deeper, we could make it down to the Haunted Cave. And we know how to get out of there. We've done it before."

"I wouldn't mind going that way," Watch said. "But I don't know which way that is." He nodded in both directions. "Do you want to go toward the light, or do you want to go toward the darkness?"

"I just want to go home," Cindy said. But she pointed in the direction of the red glow. "But we have to go that way because even if you can see in the dark, I can't."

"I agree." Watch studied his shirt sleeve. "The material is beginning to tear. My arms are swelling in size."

Cindy nodded. "You're not getting taller but you are getting more stocky. I bet pretty soon you'll be able to handle a dozen trolls."

"Don't even say it," Watch cautioned.

They started forward, in the direction of the red glow. It grew in brightness as the temperature continued to increase. Up ahead, through a haunting red haze, they glimpsed a huge room, a cavern of some kind, filled with metal equipment and dark moving shapes.

As they spotted the creatures, the creatures spotted them. Cindy and Watch heard a chorus of loud howls, and then the creatures were running toward them.

They carried spears.

And they were not human.

7

IN REALITY ADAM AND SALLY WERE NOT DEAD.
Not yet.

They had fallen a long way, far enough to break every bone in their bodies, but they had landed on the softest of all cushions, some kind of huge net. The only trouble was that it wasn't a net but a sticky web. They were alive but stuck. The net's slimy fibers held them like glue.

And they could hear the spider getting closer.

"It must be a huge creature to make a web this size," Adam said.

"It's probably poisonous as well," Sally said grimly. "Can you move?"

"Not much. How about you?"

"I'm slimed. It's all over me—in my hair, on my arms and legs. Can you see the spider yet?"

"No," Adam said. "But it's definitely moving closer."

"That's bad," Sally said.

"That's putting it mildly. Hey, I want to thank you for holding on to me when I started to fall. That was very brave of you."

"Thank you. But I think it was awfully stupid of me."

"Most brave acts are stupid," Adam agreed. He had landed on his back and there he remained—no matter how hard he tried rolling onto his side. The odor he had smelled from the grill above had become a dozen times stronger. The stink was like rotten eggs—it made it hard to breathe.

It was dark, pitch black.

They heard a slobbering sound off to their right.

They heard a munching sound off to their left.

"Oh no," Sally cried. "There are two spiders."

"Maybe they'll begin to fight over us," Adam said hopefully.

"They live together down here," Sally said. "They're not going to fight over us. We're doomed."

"Don't say that. It depresses me." Adam suddenly had an idea. "Hey, do you have your Bic lighter in your pocket?"

"Yeah. Why? Do you want to have a last smoke before you die?"

"No," Adam said. "We can use the flame to burn away the web. It's worth a try. Can you reach it?"

"I think so," Sally said as the slobbering sounds grew louder. "But if I burn away the web, we might fall farther."

"I would rather fall than be eaten," Adam said.

"That's a good point." Sally flicked on the lighter. In the light of the tiny orange flame they could see the approaching spiders. They were hideous to behold. As big as fat sheep, they had eight slimy black legs and two sharp pincers. The fire seemed to puzzle them. They stopped to stare at it with wary red eyes. But they didn't turn and flee as Adam had hoped. Green poison dripped from their ugly mouths.

The web was hanging only three feet above a black floor.

If they could burn through the web, they'd be able to stand up and escape.

"Put the flame under the web," Adam said. "See if you can get it smoking."

"I'm trying," Sally said, maneuvering the flame beneath the piece of web that gripped her right arm. To their delight, and surprise, it immediately caught fire, as hair would when put close to a lighter. The web wrinkled up quickly and released Sally's right arm. She moved the flame to the area near her left arm. The spiders made shrill angry sounds and began to move forward again.

"Hurry," Adam said. "They're coming."

"I am well aware of that fact," Sally gasped. Her left arm came free, so she was now hanging by her feet only. As she reached up to free her entangled ankles, the nearest of the spiders reached over with its pincer.

"Watch out!" Adam cried.

"Take that, you ugly creature!" Sally yelled as she suddenly pulled off her shoe and smacked the spider in the face. The spider retreated a step and screamed at the other spider. In the meantime Sally freed both her feet and dropped down to the floor, actually landing on her outstretched arms. Adam only noticed then that she looked about six years old.

"You're shrinking," he said.

Sally hurried to his side. "Do you really want to insult me at a time like this?"

"Sorry," Adam said.

Sally moved her flame to his wrists. "Pull back on the web. It burns easier when it's tight."

Adam nodded in the direction of the spiders, which had moved close to each other. It was as if the two monsters were plotting strategy. Adam didn't want to hang around to see what surprises they came up with. He pulled the web as tight as he could as Sally licked the flame over the slimy thread.

"I should carry a lighter myself," he said. "It's saved our lives a few times already."

"You get three in a pack for less than two dollars," Sally agreed.

Suddenly the spiders turned back in their direction. As a team the monsters rushed them. Adam struggled uselessly, just covering himself with more web.

"Get a stick!" he cried. "They're coming."

"We're in a dungeon. There are no sticks."

"Then get a stone!" Adam shouted as the monster moved within ten feet. "Anything! They're going to sting me with their venom!"

Sally looked around. Lying against the nearest wall were a couple of loose stones. After grabbing them she whirled on the spiders and let fly with the stones. One hit the closest spider in the eyes. The second one struck the other spider's stinger. It broke it, in fact, and the spider let out a loud miserable screech. Sally returned to melting the web as the spiders retreated to a far corner.

"I owe you one," Adam said.

"You owe me a dozen," Sally replied.

A minute later Adam was free of the sticky web and

able to stand upright on the floor beside Sally. They realized that they were not in a real dungeon. There was a wide tunnel off to the right that led out of the spider's lair. As they ran away from the web, Sally turned and shouted back at the spiders.

"Next time I'm going to bring bug spray!"

The tunnel led to a stone ladder, which was carved into the wall. The tunnel also continued farther along, but they both thought it was a good idea to head upward. But Sally was shocked to find she could hardly climb the ladder.

"It's because you're getting so short," Adam said as he came up behind her.

"I know that. You don't have to keep rubbing it in." She paused. "Hey, your voice sounds a lot deeper."

"Yeah. I sound like a teenager."

"Don't be coy," Sally said. "You sound like a man."

At the top of the stone ladder—which had been a long climb—they came to another stone tunnel. But this one was different from the others. Lit with a haunting violet light, it was much cleaner than the one they had left behind. There was also a pleasant aroma to it, as if someone had recently burned incense. Moving in the direction of the wonderful light, Adam felt as if they were entering a place of ancient magic.

"I have never seen this colored light before," Adam said.

"Yes. It's enchanting." Sally paused. "We have to be careful of another trap."

They entered a large dome-shaped chamber that was filled with bushes and trees and grass. The violet glow seemed to come out of the ceiling itself. There was even a circular pond in the room. And sitting in the middle of this tiny pool was a girl approximately ten years old, with long curly black hair. She opened her eyes as they entered, as if coming out of deep meditation. Her eyes were as green as Ann Templeton's, but the smile on her incredible face was filled with only kindness.

"Hello," she said in a gentle voice. "My name is Mireen. Who are you?"

CINDY AND WATCH HAD BEEN CAPTURED BY
a gang of huge ugly trolls. The beasts carried spears
and swords, arrows and knives. They dragged Cindy
and Watch kicking into the large cavern where more
trolls were slaving over clanging machines that made
heaven-only-knew-what. All the trolls stopped and
stared as Cindy and Watch were forced to stand beside
a pool of boiling lava. It was the lava that gave off the
red light, and perhaps helped fuel the big machines.

Cindy and Watch gave each other worried looks.
They had no doubt they were to be thrown into the
lava, or else cooked over it.

"Can you break free?" she asked in a quiet voice.

Watch shook his head. "There are too many of them."

"Silence!" one of the trolls shouted at them, poking the tip of his sword against Watch's throat. "No one gave you permission to speak."

"I'm sorry," Watch said. "I didn't know trolls spoke English."

The comment seemed to amuse the monster, for he smiled wide, and slobber fell over his breast plate of stainless steel. Like his partners', his face was blunt, his thick nose hairy, and his skin scaled, like that of a lizard. But he was bigger than his partners, and maybe that was why he was their leader. He strode in front of Watch and Cindy as if they were his trophies.

"Our boss has taught us to speak your human language," the troll said. "She says we will need it in the future, when we go out into the world, and make all of you our slaves."

"It won't happen," Cindy said. "We humans have a group called the Marines. They'll kick your ugly behinds."

The troll paused in his pacing. "Who are these Marines?"

"They are the proud and the few," Watch said. "They have much better weapons than spears and swords. If I was you guys I would stay down here. The Marines would wipe you out in one day."

"But are these Marines human?" the troll asked.

"They are human soldiers," Cindy said. "They always win, and don't quit until the enemy has been defeated." She added hopefully, "They're good friends of ours. If you hurt us, they won't like it one bit."

"Yeah, you should just let us go," Watch said. "If you eat us alive, our friends will become your enemies."

The troll snickered at their threat. "Nobody is going to save you here. We will have you for dinner, that is certain. It only remains to see how you are to be cooked." He added, "My name is Belfart by the way."

"I'm Watch and this is Cindy," Watch said.

"Pleased to meet you, Belfart," Cindy said. "Do you have to eat us? If you let us go, we promise to bring you back fresh steak from the grocery store."

Belfart scoffed. "We don't even like cows. Human meat is much more tasty." He lightly poked Cindy's side with the tip of his sword. "I think I will eat you myself."

Cindy shoved aside his sword and spat on him. "Then kill us both and get it over with. Your bad breath is giving me a headache."

Belfart wiped away the spit with his long purple tongue. "Not so fast. We have to have a vote. We are a democratic group of trolls." Belfart turned to the gathered monsters. To Cindy and Watch's surprise, he continued to speak in English, perhaps to torture them all the more. "How do we cook them?" Belfart called out.

Clearly it was an important question, at least as far as the trolls were concerned. Immediately a half-dozen of the monsters yelled out that the humans should be roasted. Just as quickly another half-dozen said that the humans should be broiled. Still others wanted them boiled, while a couple of trolls wanted them skinned alive and dropped into hot fat. Soon there was a giant argument, and Belfart had lost all control of his group. Indeed, several of the trolls drew their swords and seemed to be ready to die to defend their choice of how the humans should be cooked. Cindy glanced at Watch and sighed.

"This is worse than being eaten," Cindy said.

"I don't know about that," Watch said. "They can argue as long as they want as far as I'm concerned."

"We need a plan of action," Cindy said.

"I was going to suggest that they at least kill us before they eat us."

"That's no plan. If Adam and Sally were here, they wouldn't give up without a fight."

"If I try to fight them all," Watch said, "we'll both end up dead."

"I have an idea," Cindy said. She called over to the

troll leader. "Belfart! There's something I've got to tell you guys before you make a decision on how we're to be cooked."

Belfart shouted for the group to shut up, and because it was one of the humans who wanted to speak, they did. Cindy addressed the group as a whole.

"Now, I know you guys are hungry," she said. "And I know nothing would taste better to you than roasted human right now."

"Boiled human would taste better!" a troll shouted.

"Grilled!" another troll yelled.

"Sautéed!" a troll at the back screamed.

"Whatever!" Cindy yelled back. "You want to eat us and I can understand that. But there's something we've got to tell you guys." She paused for effect. "My partner and I are sick. If you eat us, you'll get sick too."

Belfart took a step closer and sniffed her. "You don't smell sick."

"But I am," she said. "So is Watch. We have chicken pox."

"I already had chicken pox," Watch whispered.

"And now you have them again," Cindy said quickly. "In case you think we're lying, you just have to wait a few hours and we'll get these red spots all over our bodies."

Belfart seemed unconvinced. "But we're hungry now."

"Yes," Cindy said patiently. "But you don't want to get sick. Chicken pox are awful. If you catch them, the girl trolls won't even want to get near you."

That sent a stir through the room. Belfart put his scaly hand to his fat jaw and appeared thoughtful. "How long does it take you to get the red spots?" he asked.

"We'll have them within six hours," Cindy said confidently. "Wait that long and you'll see."

"Let's wait and then fry them!" a troll shouted.

"We wait and then we bake them!" another yelled.

"No!" a bunch at the back said. "We put them in the microwave!"

"Where did they get a microwave?" Watch muttered.

"Shut up all of you!" Belfart screamed. "We will first lock them up and see if they get sick. If they don't, then we can argue about how to cook them."

Cindy leaned over and whispered in Watch's ear. "I have just bought us time."

Watch nodded grimly. "But they're just going to come for us later."

9

"I'm Adam. This is Sally," Adam said to the strange girl. "What are you doing here?"

"This is where I have always been." Mireen stood up from her patch of earth at the center of the pond. With a slight nod of her head a series of stones appeared in the water, providing a walkway for her to cross the pond. As she approached, Adam noticed she was wearing a dark gray cloak, similar in design to Ann Templeton's. She asked, "What are you doing here?"

"We've been trapped in this castle by the witch," Sally said angrily. "Has she trapped you as well?"

Mireen appeared puzzled. Her face, although very beautiful, was as pale as Ann Templeton's. It seemed almost as if it were made of marble; it didn't have a single blemish on it.

"Who is this witch you speak of?" she asked.

"Ann Templeton," Adam explained. "She gave us these magic necklaces and now we can't get them off. We can't find our way out of here either."

Mireen smiled. "Ann Templeton isn't a witch. Why do you call her that?"

"What would you call her?" Sally demanded in her now squeaky voice. Sally was down to the size of a four-year-old. In a sense, Adam wasn't doing much better. He was no longer a teenager. In fact, he seemed to have skipped his twenties altogether. He was getting really old, in his midthirties at least. Pretty soon he would have arthritis and not even be able to walk properly, like most older adults.

"I call her mother," Mireen said.

They were stunned. "You're Ann Templeton's daughter?" Sally asked.

"Yes. Don't I look like her daughter?"

Mireen did indeed resemble the witch. Yet there was an otherworldly character to her face that even Ann Templeton didn't have.

"Who's your father?" Adam asked.

A trace of sorrow touched Mireen's face. "His name is Faltoreen. But I have never met him."

"Why not?" Sally asked. "Did your mother kill him?"

"No," Mireen said. "Why would my mother kill him?"

"She's trying to kill us," Sally said.

"No, my father is alive and well," Mireen said. "He just doesn't live here."

"Where does he live?" Adam asked.

"On another planet," Mireen said. "Circling another star."

Sally laughed out loud. "I hate to tell you this, Mireen, but that's an old excuse. Your father just took off one day and didn't bother coming back. Not that I can say I blame him after seeing what's running around this castle."

"I'm not too sure of that," Adam said. "Remember how Bum said that Ann Templeton and her family were connected to star people who live in the Pleiades star cluster?"

"Pleiades," Mireen said, her face shining with pleasure at the sound of the word. "That is it. That is the name of the star cluster where my father lives."

"But you say you've never seen him," Sally said. "How come he never visits you? Doesn't he have a spaceship?"

"He commands a whole fleet of ships," Mireen said. "But my mother says it is not time for him to return here."

"I don't know if you can believe everything your mother says," Sally said.

"We explained how she's trapped us here," Adam said carefully. "You can understand that we have good reason to distrust her." He paused. "But you're more our age. We would like to trust you."

"But you're much older than me, Adam," Mireen said. "And Sally is much younger."

"We weren't when we started out today," Sally muttered.

"What Sally means is that these necklaces that we can't get off are making me older and her younger," Adam explained. "They have magic stones in them." He paused. "But maybe you know how to get them off?"

"I can certainly try," Mireen said, stepping closer. Touching Adam's necklace, she closed her eyes and became perfectly still. Under her breath she whispered a chant. Adam and Sally didn't understand a word of it. Then Mireen opened her eyes and tried to lift off the necklace. But the gold strand still would not pass over his head. Mireen added, "These are bound with powerful magic. I can't undo it, but I know my mother could."

"If she was in the mood," Sally muttered.

"Your mother said these necklaces will not come off until we find our way out of here," Adam explained. "For that reason, we have to get out of here right away.

Soon Sally will be in diapers and I'll be in my forties and unable to get around." He paused. "You do know how to get out of here, don't you?"

Mireen blinked. "No."

"But you live here," Sally said, exasperated. "You said so yourself."

"But I have never been outside," Mireen said.

"Why not?" Adam asked.

"My mother says it is not time for that, either," Mireen explained. "She says the outside is a cruel and barbaric place."

"What about the trolls in your basement?" Sally asked. "I've run into them before. They're not exactly the warm and fuzzy kind of characters."

"They are always very polite to me," Mireen said.

"What about the huge poisonous spiders you guys have?" Sally asked, trying again. "Don't tell me they like you as well."

"No, they can be troublesome. You just have to stay out of their way."

"Look," Adam said. "We don't care if you like trolls and spiders. We just want to find our friends and get out of this place."

"Where are your friends?" Mireen asked.

"We don't know," Sally said. "We got separated above

the spider's lair. The trolls could have gotten them by now for all we know."

"The trolls are not easy to control when they're hungry," Mireen admitted. "Come, we'll look for them. And after we find them, we'll search for the way out."

10

THE CELL BELFART LOCKED CINDY AND Watch in was far from pleasant. It was damp and smelly, and there was a skeleton chained to a wall in the corner. From the size of it, they figured the trolls had feasted on a kid their age earlier in the year. Perhaps as a favor, Belfart had chained them to the wall in the opposite corner.

"I wonder if it was James Hatterfield," Watch mused. "He was supposed to have disappeared in the vicinity of this castle."

"Did you go to school with him?" Cindy asked. She hadn't yet gone to school in Spooksville.

"Yeah, he was in the same grade as Sally and me. He

was a nice guy but kind of chubby." Watch added, "The trolls probably liked that."

"I still can't get over how you guys take it for granted that people disappear in this town," Cindy said.

Watch shrugged. "It happens every other day. You get used to it."

Cindy sighed. "My mother's going to be real upset if I get eaten by a troll. She wanted me home early for dinner."

"I haven't had dinner with my mother in years," Watch said quietly.

Cindy studied him in the poor light. Watch seldom talked about his family. All that Cindy knew was that his family was scattered across the country. She didn't know why.

"You miss her, don't you?" she asked.

Watch lowered his head. "Yeah, I do. I miss my father and sister, too." He raised his head. "But I can't worry about them now."

"We can talk about them later if you like," Cindy said gently. "But first we have to get out of here. Can you break your chains?"

"I was just about to try." Watch took a deep breath and tugged at the metal as hard as he could. But even though the iron pin that held the chains to the wall groaned as it moved slightly, the chains refused to come loose. Watch finally gave up straining. "Let's wait a little longer," he suggested. "I keep getting stronger. I might be able to pop them loose before the trolls come back for us."

Cindy nodded at the iron door. "But will you be able to get through that? I don't know if ten super strong men could."

Watch paused. "I think I hear someone coming."

"But it hasn't been six hours," Cindy said. "It's been less than an hour."

"Maybe trolls don't know how to tell time," Watch said.

Belfart appeared on the other side of the thick metal bars. He had a large black key with him, which he used to open the door. Stepping inside, he set aside his sword and spear, as if he wanted it to be a friendly meeting.

"It hasn't been six hours," Cindy said quickly. "You can't eat us yet."

Belfart waved away her remark. "We'll get to that later. I've come to make you a proposition."

"What kind of proposition?" Cindy asked.

"I want more information about these Marines," Belfart said. "You give it to me and I'll make sure you die painlessly."

"I have a better idea," Cindy said. "We tell you every-thing you could ever want to know about the Marines and you help us escape."

Belfart shook his head. "That's not possible. The boys are all riled up. If I let you go, they'd eat me instead. But if you do help me, at the very least I can make sure you're not sautéed."

"That's something," Watch said.

"That's ridiculous," Cindy complained. "Why should I care if I'm sautéed or barbecued if I'm dead? I'm not telling you anything about the Marines unless you let us both go. It's that simple."

"Why do you want to know about them anyway?" Watch asked.

Belfart scratched his hairy nose and paced the cell. "This is kind of hard for me to admit, being a troll and all. But when you were talking about them, something stirred deep inside me. They sound like a powerful group of boys. 'The proud and the few.' I kind of liked the sound of that." He paused. "This is strictly confiden-tial, you understand, but I would like to find out how I could join their organization."

"The Marines would never accept a troll," Watch said.

Belfart stopped pacing. His ugly face seemed to fall. "Are you sure?"

Cindy spoke quickly. "What Watch means, is they would never accept a troll with bad breath. It's against article two-three-zero of their secret code. But if you learn to brush your teeth, gargle and floss regularly, they would be happy to take you aboard."

Watch was not so sure. "Are you sure, Cindy? How would they find a uniform that fit Belfart?"

"I'm positive," Cindy said, catching Watch's eye. "In fact, why don't you give Belfart that brochure you have on the Marines."

"Which brochure is that?" Watch asked.

"The one in your back pocket," Cindy said. "If Belfart unlocks your chains, you can get it for him. Can't you, Watch?"

Watch finally caught on. His newfound muscles seemed to be making him a little slower upstairs. "Yes, I remember now. My brochure on how to get into the Marines. I would be happy to give it to you if you would just loosen these chains a little, Belfart."

Belfart paused. "This wouldn't be some kind of trick, would it?" he asked.

"What can Watch do to you?" Cindy asked. "He's just a boy, while you're a big strong handsome troll."

Belfart puffed himself up. "So you think I'm handsome?"

"I noticed it right away," Cindy said.

Belfart studied her a little closer. "Why does your skin glow?"

"It's a sign of chicken pox," Cindy muttered. "Just open Watch's chains and let him show you the best way to sign up to serve your country."

Belfart nodded enthusiastically as he took his keys back out. "I'd like to get out of here, travel some. Don't get me wrong, Ann Templeton is great to work for. It's just that I'm tired of all the back-stabbing that goes on around here. I mean, just last week an old friend tried to put a knife in me while I was taking my afternoon nap."

"There's nothing worse than a disloyal troll," Cindy said sympathetically.

"You'll find this brochure very informative," Watch promised as Belfart worked on the lock.

"Could you read it to me?" Belfart asked. "I have a little trouble understanding promotional literature."

"I'll make sure the information gets into your head," Watch said when his hands were free. He nodded to the chains on his feet. "Could you get those as well? It's hard for me to get to my back pocket while I'm still pinned to the wall."

Belfart was in a trusting mood. "No problem," he said, bending over. "You guys are more polite than most of the humans we've seen around here. Most of them refuse to stop screaming and begging. It gets on your nerves after a while. You just want to put them in the pot even if it means in the end you don't get the meat flavored exactly the way you want it."

"We are very polite," Cindy said, nodding to Watch.

"You can trust us with your life," Watch said as he brought his hands up above Belfart's head. The troll had just snapped the ankle chains free, and was glancing up, when Watch brought his fists down hard. Watch was plenty strong by now. It was a loud blow. He almost took off the troll's head.

Belfart crumpled unconscious to the floor.

"Grab his keys," Cindy said, excited. "Undo my chains. We can be out of here before he wakes up."

Watch reached for the keys. "I have a better idea. Let's take him as a hostage."

"Do you think you can handle him?" Cindy asked.

"If I keep a sword to his throat I can. He may even know a way out of here."

Cindy looked down at the sleeping troll and frowned. "I don't know. He doesn't look as if he gets out much."

11

THE POWER OF THE MAGIC NECKLACES WAS still at work. Adam was now an old man, at least fifty, and Sally was as small as a two-year-old. Adam had to carry her in his arms as Mireen led them through the castle, just so they could both keep up. Sally didn't like being carried. She kept bothering Adam about his diaper remark.

"I'm not wearing them," she said. "I don't care how young I get. And you're certainly not changing them."

"You might have to wear them," Adam said. "Look at you now. You've slipped out of your pants. Your shirt is the only thing covering you up."

"I like this shirt," Sally said. "It's one of my favorites.

But I mean what I say. I don't want some senile old goat taking care of me when I'm a baby."

"I'm not senile yet," Adam said.

"But you're getting close. Your hair's almost white."

"It's silver, it's not white."

"See," Sally said. "You're too far gone to know there's no difference."

"Do you two always argue like this?" Mireen asked.

"Yes," Sally said.

"No," Adam said, then sighed. "Sometimes. Look, do you know where you're going?"

"I know my way around the castle," Mireen explained. "But it's a big place, and I have no idea where your friends might be. I'm just looking everywhere."

"Let's try searching the troll's basement," Sally said. "Knowing Cindy and Watch, they're probably being roasted alive as we speak."

"We can look there if you'd like," Mireen said, stopping in front of a stone wall and muttering a few words of magic. There didn't seem to be many real doors in the place. Mireen was forever materializing passageways out of nothing. This time was no exception. A narrow doorway suddenly appeared before them and they hurried inside. Glancing over his shoulder, Adam saw the wall reappear where it had been. The path before them was dark but that didn't seem to bother Mireen.

"Do you have any idea where your mother is?" he asked Mireen.

"If she is in the castle, she is hiding from even me," Mireen said, troubled. "I can usually find her just by thinking about her."

"She might be testing you as well as us," Adam said.

"Testing me?" Mireen said. "I don't understand."

"The witch"—Sally began—"I mean, your mother said she was testing us with these necklaces."

Mireen continued to appear troubled. "Are all the kids outside afraid of my mother?"

"Most of them," Adam admitted. "She is supposed to have murdered a lot of them."

Mireen laughed, but it sounded forced. "My mother would never murder anyone. How can those kids be so foolish?"

"They've lost too many brothers and sisters?" Sally suggested.

Mireen shook her head. "My mother's powerful, but she never abuses her power. There is a reason for everything she does."

"I hope you're right," Adam muttered.

"Tell me what it's like on the outside," Mireen said.

"In Spooksville or in the world as a whole?" Sally asked. "The reason I ask is because Spooksville is unlike any other place. Other cities don't have castles like this."

"What do you do each day for fun?" Mireen asked.

"Before I moved here from Kansas City," Adam said, "I used to go swimming and fishing in the lake. Sometimes I would ride my bike and play baseball."

"But since he got here he's been struggling to stay alive," Sally said. "We wrestle with ghosts, fight with aliens, destroy cold creatures from the past, get lost in haunted caves. We have all kinds of fun. It's a laugh a minute. You should play with us sometime. You're more than welcome."

"Perhaps someday I will," Mireen said in a soft, maybe sad, voice.

"Do you have anyone to play with?" Adam asked gently.

"I have learned to play in my imagination," Mireen said. "My mother says that's the best place to play. There are more possibilities inside us, she says, than outside."

"Hmm," Adam muttered thoughtfully. "Those are beautiful words."

"And of absolutely no use to us now," Sally said. "Sorry, Mireen, but if we don't get these necklaces off soon, you won't be playing with us. You'll be babysitting us."

"I will do everything I can to help you," Mireen promised.

They passed from their narrow passageway into a wider tunnel lit with a sober red glow. In the distance they could hear frantic steps, two or three people running their way. But beyond that, a little farther away, they could hear what sounded like a small army of trolls in battle gear. Adam strained his eyes to see in the gloomy light. One of the approaching figures seemed to be glowing. Adam realized who he was looking at.

"Cindy!" Adam called. "Watch! We're over here!"

12

CINDY AND WATCH CAUGHT UP TO THEM A few minutes later. Adam was surprised to see they had a troll with them. Watch guarded the monster by holding a sword to the troll's throat, but the troll didn't seem to mind. In fact, he offered his hand.

"I'm Belfart," he said. "I'm a Marine."

"I'm Mireen," Mireen said to Cindy and Watch.

"She's the witch's daughter," Sally said.

"Wow," Watch said. "I didn't know Ann Templeton was even married."

"Belfart wants to be a Marine," Cindy explained impatiently. "But let's drop these introductions. We can do that later. What are you guys doing here? You're supposed to be dead."

"Don't count the dead in this town until you've seen the bodies," Sally said.

"I'll never do it again." Cindy hugged them both. "I'm just so happy to see you guys are all right."

"Yeah, this is great," Watch said with unexpected emotion in his voice. He reached over and hugged them too. But they just ended up crushing little Sally. She pushed them away.

"This is not great," she said. "I can hardly walk anymore. And you, Watch, you look ready to burst out of your clothes. Adam's got the same problem, mind you. Mireen had to find him a sheet to keep him covered. And you, Cindy, you're so radiant you're on the verge of disappearing."

"I know that," Cindy said. "We have to get these necklaces off."

"First we have to get away from these trolls who are chasing us," Watch said. "We just escaped from their prison and they're real mad."

"I'll talk to them," Mireen said. "They won't hurt you."

"If I may beg to differ, my lady," Belfart said, "you won't calm them down by talking to them. I know my boys. They want human meat and they want it now. They don't even care how it's cooked, and that tells you how upset they are."

"But can't you calm them down?" Mireen asked.

Belfart rubbed his head and glanced at Cindy and Watch. "They think I helped these guys escape. They're hot for my bones as well."

"Can't you lead us into a secret passageway?" Adam asked Mireen.

"Can't she just lead us out of here?" Cindy asked.

"That's what I asked," Sally muttered.

"There is no secret passageway here," Mireen said. "We have to go farther up the tunnel."

"But we just came out of a secret passageway," Adam said.

"Yes, but it was a one-way passageway," Mireen explained. "Come, let's hurry. I know a place to take you where you will be safe."

"Will there be a bottle there for Sally?" Cindy teased.

"Shut up," Sally grumbled.

They ran up the tunnel as best as they could, but the trolls continued to gain on them. Adam had handed Sally to Watch to carry, but he was still slowing down the group. He definitely had arthritis now. His knees and hips ached. Plus, breathing was hard. Running a few steps winded him. He estimated he was seventy years old.

Cindy was also having trouble running. It was as if her disappearing feet couldn't grip the ground. She bounced in the air as she ran, as if she were on the moon.

Behind them, the troll army became visible, dozens of burning eyes.

"The boys are full of life tonight," Belfart said wistfully. "Better get us to a passageway quick, my lady, or they'll tear us apart in this very tunnel."

"We still have a ways to go," Mireen said anxiously.

"You're a witch's daughter," Sally said. "Do some witchcraft. Scare them away."

Mireen stopped. "There is a spell I know that might slow them down." She put her hands to her head as if thinking deeply. "But I can't remember exactly how it goes."

"Is there a pocket witch dictionary or something you can look in?" Sally asked.

"Let her concentrate," Adam said. "There's no hurry, Mireen. Take your time."

"But don't take too much of it," Belfart said.

Cindy nodded to Watch. "He's definitely Marine material."

"I got it!" Mireen said, excited. "I think I've got it. All of you, stand back."

They cleared a space for her as she stepped into the center of the tunnel and faced in the direction of the approaching army. The trolls were clearly visible now, and they were not a pleasant sight. They had their swords drawn, and even the sight of their boss's daughter didn't slow them one bit. Unless Mireen was able to stop them, Adam realized, the horde would be on them in a minute.

"Katuu Shamar Plean!" Mireen called as she lifted her arms.

Nothing happened.

"Try another one," Sally said anxiously.

Mireen closed her eyes and drew in a deep breath. She raised her arms. "Katuu Shamar Klean!"

The tunnel burst into fire. The flames exploded out of thin air in front of the attacking trolls. Adam was not sure if any of them got burned, but the whole bunch of them sure got scared. They turned and ran the other way.

But then the flames went out.

"Do it again!" Sally called from her place in Watch's strong arms.

"I can do it only once," Mireen said wearily as she turned and stumbled up the tunnel. "That was enough to drain all my power."

"That won't hold them for long, my lady," Belfart said. "Best we find that secret passageway quickly."

Belfart was right. Already a few of the trolls looked as if they were having second thoughts about leaving their dinner. Several were still staring their way, calling to their partners to come back. Adam braced himself for another exhausting dash. If the trolls didn't get him, he thought, a heart attack would. He had never realized how miserable it could be to grow old.

They hurried up the tunnel, Adam staggering, Cindy bouncing, Mireen stumbling, and Sally complaining. Only Watch seemed in good shape. In a sense, his necklace had done him the most good. At least he seemed to be experiencing the fewest side effects.

Behind them, the trolls regrouped and started after them again.

"Is it much farther?" Adam gasped.

"We're almost there," Mireen called. "I think."

Another exhausting five minutes went by. Adam struggled on as best as he could, but invariably he began to fall behind the others. But faint whistling sounds in the dark gave him an unlooked for burst of energy. The trolls were firing arrows at him, trying to cut him down. Adam swore he wouldn't give them the pleasure.

Up ahead, Mireen stopped and faced the stone wall.

The gang gathered around her. Adam was just coming up when an opening appeared out of nowhere. As a group, they poured into the magic doorway. Arrows bounced on the stone above their heads.

"Close it!" Adam cried when they were all inside.

"Weeta!" Mireen shouted over her shoulder.

The doorway vanished. The trolls were stopped.

The gang staggered through the passageway.

Then they exited into a large room.

Adam recognized it. The room with the hourglass.

The witch was waiting for them.

13

"So you still haven't found your way out," Ann Templeton said, her back to the magic hourglass. The light of the stardust shone around her, creating a colored aura over her head. To Adam she didn't even look human anymore, more like a powerful being from another solar system. Her green eyes glittered as she spoke, as if with strong emotion, even though her voice remained calm. She added, "What does this mean?"

"It means you need more doors in this joint," Sally said.

Ann Templeton smiled and gestured in the direction of the hallway through which they had first entered the room. "Why don't you go that way?" she asked. "See what you can find?"

Adam took a weary step forward. "We know we would find nothing. You have us locked in a maze. There is no way out. Even your own daughter does not know how to get out of this place."

Mireen also took a step forward. "Why are you torturing these nice kids?"

"Be silent, Mireen," Ann Templeton said. "Watch, listen, learn."

"No," Mireen replied. "I can't remain silent while my friends are in danger."

Her daughter's defiance seemed to surprise Ann Templeton, to anger her even. But she quickly mastered her emotions. She spoke in a quiet voice.

"You just met these people. How can you call them friends?"

Mireen shook her head. "It's just how I feel. I like them, I care about them." She added reluctantly, "I can't let you hurt them."

Ann Templeton smiled coldly. "Do I hurt them? I did not ask them to come here. They wanted to. They wanted to see what my castle was like. Now they know. Now they're happy."

"I wouldn't exactly say that I'm a happy one-year-old," Sally muttered in a babylike voice.

Adam spoke with effort. He still hadn't caught his

breath from the mad dash up the tunnel. "You must know that we're running out of time. Soon Cindy will disappear, Sally will turn back into an egg, and I'll die of old age. If we've failed your test, then we've failed it. We don't know what else we can do to get out of here."

"Why, Adam, I'm disappointed in you," Ann Templeton said in a serious voice. "You have not even tried to get out of here. Sure, you've crawled into this hole, and explored this cave, and searched through this passageway. But that is not how you escape from a trap. To do that you have to look at how you got into the trap. Then you will know what to do."

"But, Mother," Mireen pleaded. "Adam told you. They don't have time for this. They're dying."

"How do you feel, Watch?" Ann Templeton asked. "Do you feel like you're dying?"

"No, ma'am," he replied. "I feel stronger than ever."

"Somehow I'm not surprised." Ann Templeton lowered her head and closed her eyes, as if thinking deeply. Then she raised her head and stared at each one of them, including her daughter. Finally she spoke, and there was great power in her words, as if she were passing judgment on them. "I will leave you now. You will pass the test or you will fail it. It is up to you." She turned away. "Come, Mireen."

"No," her daughter said flatly. "I'm staying here with my friends. If you won't help them, maybe I can."

Ann Templeton paused and studied her. But she seemed unconcerned with her daughter's disobedience. "You're old enough to make up your own mind, Mireen." She gestured to Belfart. "Come with me."

"See you guys later," he said casually. "If I'm lucky. Remember that brochure on the Marines. I still think they could use a few good trolls."

And with that Ann Templeton and Belfart vanished into the wall.

14

"SHE SURE MAKES A STUNNING EXIT, DOESN'T she?" Sally said in her baby voice.

Adam stepped to the hourglass and leaned against it for support. "We're back where we started from."

"No," Cindy disagreed in a voice they could hardly hear. They could see right through her now. Her words were like a ghost's whispers. "We're worse off than when we started. We have only a few minutes left to figure out what to do."

Adam sighed. "I just wish I could think clearer. I'm definitely getting senile. Does anyone have any suggestions?"

"The witch did not have to meet us here," Watch said. "But she did, and I think she did so as a favor."

"I could do with less of her favors," Sally said.

"You misunderstand me," Watch said. "I think she was trying to give us a hint. Let's think about what she said. 'But that is not how you escape from a trap. To do that you have to look at how you got into the trap. Then you will know what to do.'" Watch paused. "The key must be in those words."

"But how did we get in this trap?" Adam asked. "We walked over and walked inside and we were trapped."

"No," Cindy said. "The door closed behind us as soon as we stepped inside, but I don't think we were trapped until we put on the necklaces. The witch said as much earlier."

"I think we have to go farther back than that," Watch said. "I think we have to ask ourselves why we came here."

"For the usual reasons," Sally said. "Because we were bored and stupid."

"We may have been bored," Adam said. "But the thing that made us decide to come here was Watch's failing eyesight."

"And Watch is the only one who is not suffering right now," Mireen said. "Mother pointed that out. She said that it did not surprise her."

"But why isn't Watch suffering like the rest of us?" Cindy said. "Maybe that's the key to this big test."

"I think he's going to suffer when he tries to buy some new clothes," Sally said. "Already he looks like the Incredible Hulk."

"Cindy's onto something," Adam interrupted. "We came here because of Watch. Actually, Watch was the only one who had a genuine reason to come. He needed help with his eyesight and now his eyesight is better. Also, he was the first one to put on the necklace. He trusted that he would be all right. He had faith."

"Thank you for the sermon," Sally said. "But how does this help us get these stupid necklaces off?"

"I think it gives us a clue as to why we can't get them off," Adam said. "I put the necklace on because I wanted something for nothing. I wanted to be more mature."

"And I wanted to be prettier," Cindy agreed. "Even though I was pretty enough to begin with."

"And humble enough," Sally added.

"The point is the three of us were fine to begin with," Adam said. "We didn't have anything wrong with us. But still we put on the necklaces." He paused. "Could the test be just that? That we took something we didn't need. That we were fine the way we were and we still wanted something more."

Cindy nodded. "I think that's it. The test is inside. It's there that we failed it."

"But how do we get these stupid necklaces off?" Sally demanded.

Mireen spoke up. "My mother has a saying. It's always been one of my favorites. She says that the things we crave the most destroy us the quickest."

"Interesting," Adam said thoughtfully. "I certainly don't crave maturity anymore."

"And I don't crave beauty anymore," Cindy said.

They all looked at little Sally.

"Well, I'm tired of being a baby if that's what you want to hear," she said. "Now I have just one tiny question. I've asked it before. How do we get these necklaces off?"

They stared at one another, searching for an answer.

"Why don't you just try taking them off?" Mireen suggested.

"We tried that already," Sally said. "Many times. They won't come off."

"Try now," Mireen said gently.

Adam tried first.

Without effort, the necklace passed over his head.

Cindy quickly pulled off her necklace.

Sally took hers off. She smiled a big baby smile.

They all stared at Watch. He fingered his ruby.

"You don't have to take it off," Adam said. "It isn't hurting you."

Watch was doubtful. "But how can I want to be special when you guys aren't allowed to be? It's not fair." He pulled the necklace over his head. "I got by before. I can get by again. Even if I do go blind, there are worse things."

Mireen went over and put her hand on Watch's chest. "You're a great person. You have a big heart."

Watch blushed. "Thank you."

"I think this may be the start of something," Cindy said.

"Excuse me," Sally spoke up. "Are you guys forgetting a minor detail? We have removed the necklaces and maybe we have stopped aging and shrinking and disappearing. But we are still far from normal."

"I think I may have an answer to that problem," Adam said, touching the hourglass once more. "Mireen, has your mother ever spoken about this hourglass?"

"Very seldom," Mireen said. "But she did once say that its power reached to the stars. That even the stars' paths through the heavens could be influenced by it."

"What does that mean?" Sally said.

"We already know," Adam said. "We were shown on the other side of the Secret Path. This hourglass controls the flow of time."

"But you said we can't mess with it," Cindy said. "You said it could destroy our world."

"I said we couldn't destroy it," Adam corrected. "We destroyed the other one in the other dimension. But what if we perform an experiment. What if we put the necklaces back on, and turn the hourglass upside down, and then see what happens."

"What will happen?" Cindy asked.

Watch understood. "Time will begin to flow backward. The effect of the necklaces on us might begin to reverse."

"It's a possibility," Adam said. "I can't guarantee anything."

"I say we try it," Sally said. "I think I'm going to be needing a diaper soon."

"How cute," Cindy said.

"Don't joke," Sally warned.

"This hourglass weighs a ton," Mireen said. "How will we turn it over?"

Watch flexed his muscles. "No problem. I can lift it up with one hand."

"But Mireen has a point," Adam warned. "If our experiment works, we'll have to turn the hourglass back around. Then you won't be super strong anymore, Watch. We might get trapped in a time warp, where we have to live our lives backward."

"I refuse to go through all my psychological crises over again," Sally said. "I just finished with that junk."

"We can worry about that when we come to it," Watch said.

"I would rather worry about it now," Adam said.

Watch did something unusual then. He reached out and touched Adam's shoulder. He held his friend's eye.

"Adam," he said. "A moment ago you said I had faith. That's why I wasn't hurt by my necklace. Well, I have faith right now. If we do this, everything will work out. Ann Templeton will know we have passed our test. She will help us if we need the help."

"You really think so?" Adam asked. "After all she's put us through, you still think she's a good witch?"

Watch didn't hesitate. "I'm sure of it."

"So am I," Mireen added. "She may be a witch to you guys, but she's still my mother. I trust her."

"Okay," Adam said, putting his necklace back on. "Let's do it. Let's see if we can't get ourselves back to normal."

With the exception of Mireen, each of them put a necklace back on. Watch approached the glowing hourglass. He was as strong as he looked. In one smooth move, he inverted the magical timekeeper.

Now the sparkling stardust began to flow *upward*.

A wave of drowsiness swept over Adam. He blinked, trying to rub it from his eyes, but noticed he was not alone with his tired feelings. Each of them was slumping slowly to the ground. Now they really were in the witch's hands.

There was nothing Adam could do.

The drowsiness was too hard to resist.

He closed his eyes and blacked out.

Epilogue

THAT EVENING, WHILE ENJOYING MILK AND doughnuts at their favorite coffee shop, they traded stories about what they experienced after the hourglass had been inverted. But basically all their stories were the same. They had fallen asleep and awakened outside beside the castle, in the same shape as when they entered the castle. They'd had another great adventure, but nothing had changed.

Or had it?

Mireen had not been with them when they had awakened.

"But maybe now her mother will let her come out

and play sometimes," Cindy said. "I imagine Mireen will want to see us again."

"I want to see her again," Watch said quietly.

Sally shoved his side. "You don't have a crush on her, do you, Watch?"

"No," he said quickly.

"That would spoil your cool and detached image," Adam teased.

Watch smiled to himself. "She didn't want to change my image too much."

"Who is she?" Sally asked. "What are you talking about?"

"Ann Templeton," Watch said. "She actually woke me before you guys, when we were still inside the castle. I don't know if she wants me to talk about it, but I guess it's all right."

"What did she say to you?" Adam asked.

"Not much. She just told me to take off my necklace."

They all jumped. "Then you stopped the reversal process!" Cindy exclaimed. "You can see without your glasses." She paused. "But you still have your glasses on."

Watch nodded. "I had reversed to almost how I was before I entered the castle. She told me that was for the best, for now. But she did allow my eyes to be improved enough so that I won't keep bumping into things."

"That's a miracle," Cindy said. "You must be grateful."

"I am," Watch said shyly.

"Wait a second," Sally said. "I would be angry with her. She could have at least awakened you early enough so that you wouldn't have to wear glasses at all. For that matter, she should have given you the necklace. She promised it to us if we passed the test. If anyone passed it, Watch, I think it was you."

Watch smiled and shook his head. "She said she didn't want to do that."

"Why not?" Sally demanded.

"She said I looked better in glasses," Watch said simply.

Sally thought for a moment as she stared at her friend.

Then she, too, smiled. It was a happy smile.

"For once I agree with her," Sally said.

TURN THE PAGE FOR A SNEAK PEAK AT
SPOOKVILLE #7: THE DARK CORNER

IT WAS SALLY WILCOX WHO BROUGHT UP how cool Bryce Poole was and started the argument that led to their taking another trip through the Secret Path. Of course she later swore she had nothing to do with what happened. It was typical. No one, especially Sally, ever wanted to be blamed for starting an adventure, at least not in the middle of the adventure—when it looked like they would all die.

The day started as so many did that summer in Springville, known as Spooksville to all the town kids. Adam Freeman, Cindy Makey, Sally Wilcox, and Watch were together for a breakfast of milk and doughnuts. While stuffing their faces at the local coffee shop, they tried to figure out what to do with the day.

"Only a few weeks and we'll be back in school," Sally said, brushing her brown bangs out of her eyes. "We have to make the most of every day."

"I'm kind of looking forward to starting school here," Cindy, who was new to town, said. "I like learning things."

"Summer vacation in Spooksville is more of a learning experience than anything we do in school," Sally muttered.

"What is school like here?" Adam, who was also new to town, asked. "Is it as weird as the rest of the town?"

"It's pretty normal," Watch said.

"Except for a few of the teachers," Sally added. "The ones that aren't human."

"How did I know you were going to say that?" Cindy asked.

"There are a couple of unusual teachers in the middle school," Watch admitted.

Sally nodded. "There's Mr. Castro. He teaches history, basically. But sometimes he talks about the future."

"Don't say it," Cindy interrupted, flipping her long blond hair over a shoulder. "Mr. Castro's really from the future."

"Well, he's not from around here," Watch said.

"I think he was built at the North Pole," Sally said. "If my sources are accurate."

"I heard it was the South Pole," Watch said.

Adam and Cindy exchanged looks. "So he's a robot?" Adam asked.

"He's not a desktop computer," Sally said.

Watch spoke reluctantly. "He does seem to have several machinelike qualities. For example, he never eats lunch. He never drinks water. When he's tired, he lays out on the football field and soaks up the sun's rays. I guess that's how he recharges his batteries."

"He also has a hearing aid that looks more like a cosmic receiver," Sally said. "He never takes it off. I hear it's wired directly into his positronic brain." She added, "He sure doesn't have trouble hearing."

Cindy shook her head. "I don't believe any of this."

"Wait till you get him for history," Sally said. "And he pops his eyes out in the middle of a lecture just to clean his contact lenses."

"You said a couple of teachers were weird," Adam said. "Who's the other one?"

"Mrs. Fry," Sally said. "She teaches biology. She's a snake."

"She has scaly skin?" Cindy asked.

"Yes," Sally said impatiently. "I told you, she's a snake.

When have you ever seen a snake that didn't have scaly skin?"

"What Sally means is Mrs. Fry seems to be part snake," Watch said. "She slides around the room and hisses all the time. Some people think she's a descendant of a reptilian race that lived here millions of years ago."

"Frogs are dissected all the time in her class," Sally said. "But never snakes or lizard. And all the frog parts—well, they disappear between classes. She eats them all."

Cindy made a face. "That's gross."

"You haven't seen gross until you've seen Mrs. Fry shed her skin," Sally said.

Adam didn't know what to make of any of this. "It sounds like it's going to be an interesting school year."

Sally brightened. "There are some cute guys at school."

Cindy was cautious. "Are they human?"

Sally waved her hand. "There's this one guy, his name's Bryce Poole, and he's so cool. He's like a young James Bond. Nothing disturbs him. You'll adore him, Cindy. He's got real dark hair, and super warm brown eyes. He's only twelve but he doesn't act like a kid. He talks like a well-read, sophisticated adult—like me."

Cindy was interested. "How come we haven't seen him this summer?"

"He's a loner," Sally said in a confidential tone. "He

takes his own risks and he doesn't go whining to anyone about the consequences."

"It's hard to imagine anyone who's taken more risks than we did this summer," Adam muttered.

"And I can't remember that we ever whined to anyone," Watch added.

Sally stopped and laughed. "Are you guys jealous of Bryce?"

Adam shrugged. "How can I be jealous of someone I've never met?"

"I've met him and he's no big deal," Watch said.

"What bothers you guys more?" Sally persisted. "Is it his obvious intelligence? His smoldering good looks? Or is it his dynamic attitude?"

"I told you," Adam said, "I've never met the guy. I know nothing about him."

"I'm trying to tell you about him," Sally said. "And you're getting all upset." She paused. "I think you're jealous, but you don't have to be. I like him as a friend. There's nothing between us."

"I bet he's wonderful," Cindy gushed.

"How can you say that?" Adam, who was a little insecure about his looks and especially about his height, demanded. "You haven't met him either."

"But if Cindy does fall in love with him when she

meets him," Sally said, "you mustn't stand in her way, Adam. You have to be mature about it. So Bryce is better-looking, taller, and smarter than you and Watch. It doesn't mean you're not worthy human beings."

"Oh brother," Adam muttered.

"Where's a good place to meet him?" Cindy asked.

Sally spoke seriously. "You have to catch him coming or going. He never stays in one place long. He's always taking some super risk to protect this town from danger."

"Hold on a second," Adam said. "Since I've been here, what has he done to protect this town? I mean, where was he when we had to deal with aliens, the Haunted Cave, the Cold People, not to mention the witch. Where was he all this time?"

"Yeah," Watch agreed. "Bryce didn't even bother to help us out with the Howling Ghost."

Sally smiled condescendingly. "Bryce doesn't deal with small crises. He only handles major ones."

"How can you call the Cold People a small crisis?" Adam demanded. "If we hadn't stopped them, they would have taken over the whole planet."

"Yes, but this isn't that big a planet," Sally said. "Not compared to the rest of the galaxy. Bryce deals more with cosmic emergencies."

"I thought you said he protected the town," Adam interrupted.

"And many other places," Sally said.

Adam and Watch looked at each other and rolled their eyes. "Like what kind of cosmic emergencies?" Adam tried again. "What is this big shot Bryce doing right now to protect us?"

Sally glanced around the coffee shop to make sure no one was listening. She spoke in a hushed tone. "Bryce is working with the Secret Path. He's trying to halt the interdimensional flow of negativity so that it doesn't seep into our reality."

Adam frowned. "How do you know this?"

Sally sat back and nodded gravely. "I have my sources."

"I don't believe it," Watch said. "Bryce Poole doesn't even know what the Secret Path is. I asked him about it once and he didn't even know where it began."

"He was just acting like he didn't know," Sally said. "After I told him about our adventures on the other side of it, he told me he didn't think you were equipped enough to survive the dangers of the interdimensional portal."

It was Watch's turn to frown. "Equipped with what?"

"I don't want to get personal here," Sally said.

"You are always personal," Adam said dryly.

Sally was offended. "Don't take it out on me because Cindy is suddenly interested in another guy."

"I didn't say I was interested," Cindy said.

"Your voice said it all," Sally corrected. "And I understand what Adam's going through. I'm sympathetic. To experience raging jealously and bitter rejection for the first time is not easy."

Adam sighed. "I am so grateful for your sympathy."

"We're arguing about nothing," Watch said. "Bryce isn't a super hero. He's probably not ever used the Secret Path."

"How do you know?" Sally shot back. "You've been afraid to use it since that first time."

"I haven't been afraid," Watch said. "I've just been busy with other things."

"Yeah, like saving the planet with me, his best friend," Adam added.

"I saved the planet, too," Sally said.

"Then you and Bryce should be perfect together," Adam said.

Sally laughed. "You are so jealous!"

Adam got angry. "Why should I be jealous of a guy who thinks he's James Bond? I agree with Watch. This guy has not been on the Secret Path. He doesn't have the guts."

Sally stood. "Why don't we go see?"

"Go where?" Cindy asked. "See what? What is the Secret Path?"

"It winds through town and leads to other dimensions," Watch explained.

"It starts or ends in the cemetery," Sally added. "Depending on how you look at it. Why don't we go there and look for signs of Bryce? Then we can see who the real hero in this town is."

"Why would Bryce leave signs that he's been using the Secret Path?" Watch asked.

"Yeah," Adam said. "Who is he trying to impress?"

"You guys have an answer for everything." Sally snickered and turned for the door. "Are you chickens coming or not?"

The way she worded the question, it was impossible to say no.

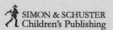